HOCUS POCUS PRACTICE FOCUS

The Making of a Magician

WRITTEN BY AMY KIMLAT
ILLUSTRATED BY SRINIDHI SRINIVASAN

Foreword by David Copperfield

FLOATING MATCH

PRESS

FOR MOM, WHO HELPED ME WITH MY FIRST MAGIC SHOW
FOR ESTELLE & ADELAIDE, WHO ADD WONDER INTO EVERY MOMENT
AND FOR KOSTYA, WHO BRINGS THE MAGIC INTO MY LIFE

ISBN 978-1-958573-00-6 (hardback)
ISBN 978-1-958573-01-3 (paperback)
ISBN 978-1-958573-02-0 (e-book)

Conjured in Winter Park, Florida

FLOATING MATCH
PRESS
www.floatingmatchpress.com

A MESSAGE FROM DAVID COPPERFIELD

To the Magician's Parent:

When my daughters were younger, they never preferred the characters with the longest hair, the biggest bows, or the brightest dresses.

No, my girls preferred the heroines with powers. Magical, extraordinary, wondrous powers.

And we see so many examples of these strong, magical women throughout our literary history — from snow queens to fairy godmothers.

So why has magic, as a professional field, been so dominated by men?

Thankfully, the magic world is evolving. More women are selling out theaters, headlining Vegas shows, and winning TV competitions.

And yet, women have performed magic professionally for centuries. My private magic museum in Las Vegas houses hundreds of pictures, posters, and props belonging to women in magic, past and present.

But we need to do more to shine a light on these successful women in magic — and we need to do it right from the start. Young girls need to see that magic is not just a possibility for them — it's a reality.

Hocus Pocus Practice Focus shares this reality through its characters, Mila, the kid magician, and Greta the Great, the professional. **That's why this is a book that every child interested in magic should have and every girl interested in magic needs.**

Through Mila's journey into magic, Amy Kimlat reveals some of my most important secrets. But these secrets aren't the technical methods behind my magic.

Instead, they're what I call the three Ps of success — passion, preparation, and persistence.

Mila's path into magic teaches kids that success comes only through deep commitment, intense study, and plucky persistence.

These are the truly magical, extraordinary, and wondrous powers — the powers that we, as parents, hope our children will carry with them, forever.

David Copperfield
Dad & Magician

When Mila woke up, she declared, "I'm awake!"
For today was the day for her party with cake!

Soon after they'd put out the birthday supplies,
Mila's mom and dad told her,
"We have a Surprise!"

A woman swept in as her friends sat and ate.
Then they cheered when she said,
"I am Greta the Great!"

"I am here to **delight** you, **amaze**, and **perplex**.
Mila, join me to help with the magic effects!"

First, Greta began with a "HOCUS!" and "POCUS!"
Then from nowhere, she pulled a bouquet into focus!

Next, Greta poured juice from her pitcher's wide spout

in a tube of rolled paper, and nothing leaked out!

Then Greta the Great cut a rope into two,

which she put back together without any glue!

Last, Greta laid Mila on top of two chairs.
When she took out just one, Mila stayed in the air!

Her friends cheered and clapped as she giggled with glee.
Then she thought to herself...

"Just how hard can this be?"

When her friends all went home, she knew just what to do.
She stood tall and said,

"I'M a magician
now, TOO! "

Mila told all her stuffies
to watch on her bed,
"I am here to amaze you,
my stuffies," she said.

Mila turned to her bunny,
commanding, "Sit down!"

Then she pulled
out his chair,
and he crashed
to the ground!

She continued, exclaiming, "The show must go on!"
So she grabbed her sweet dolly whose face she had drawn.

Mila snipped, and she snipped 'til her doll split in two,

but she then had two halves and no clue what to do!

The next day, Mila shouted,

"HEY! WATCH MY NEW TRICK!"

The she rolled up her homework and yelled, "I'll be quick!"

She squealed, "HOCUS!" then "POCUS!" and poured in her punch.

But the sweet, sticky juice spilled on everyone's lunch!

Her friends all looked stunned as they looked at the mess.
Then she realized her teacher had juice on her dress.
Mila knew this was bad when she furrowed her brow...

"Mila, go get a mop and
please clean this mess now."

"I will never delight or perplex or amaze,"
Mila cried to herself, "I am done with this phase.
I became a magician to get lots of cheers,
but I have no powers," she said through her tears.

The principal heard Mila's cries of despair.
"Mila, no one has powers, they all just prepare.

Magicians work hard, just like dancers and singers.

They don't become great just by snapping their fingers."

As she thought about this,
Mila felt so confused.
"They prepare?" Mila asked.
Ms. McGee looked amused.
"But how do you know?"
Mila couldn't think straight.
Then Ms. McGee whispered...

I'm Greta the Great.

LUNCH ROOM

Mila couldn't believe Ms. McGee had her fooled!
HERE WAS GRETA THE GREAT AS THE
HEAD OF HER SCHOOL!

"I am sure that to you
this is quite the surprise,
but to get my work done,
I must stay in disguise!"

"You performed
at my house?"

Mila tried
to recall.

"Yes, the flowers, the floating, the pouring, and all!
You will have to first study and **practice** and **focus**,
Before jumping on stage to shout,
"HOCUS!" or "POCUS!"

"But where can I learn?" Mila thought to herself. And she quickly imagined a book on a shelf. "At the library! Yes! I'll learn magic tricks there! Yes, the library has what I need to prepare!"

Mila hoped that she'd find the one book that she'd need,
but she left with a magic book pile to read!

Mila stayed up all night, as if she was on stage,
trying over and over one trick from one page.

At school, Mila practiced her magic technique.

Ms. McGee was impressed and suggested a tweak.

She was feeling encouraged and practiced most nights,
entertaining her family with all of her sleights.

Mila wanted to quit when she didn't have answers,

but she just needed practice like singers and dancers.

So she studied, rehearsed, and improved with each try, until Mila was older. A year had gone by!

Mila leapt out of bed. "It's the day!" she declared. For today she'd present everything she'd prepared.

She beamed, "HOCUS" then "POCUS" without any fear,

And made all of her sweet, sticky juice disappear.

Her bunny was floating...

...her dolly stayed whole.

Thanks to practice she kept all her nerves in control.

Proudly, Mila delighted, amazed, and perplexed all her guests with her wonderful magic effects!

Her friends cheered and clapped at her birthday event, but today they cheered

MILA ... THE MAGNIFICENT!!

MAKE A TOOTHPICK DISAPPEAR!

By Mila the Magnificent

The first magic trick I learned to perform was The Disappearing Toothpick! I practiced this trick over and over again while standing in front of the bathroom mirror, so I could see what my audience sees. I'm going to teach you how to perform this trick right now!

WHAT YOU'LL NEED:

- A small piece of clear tape
- A toothpick (Don't have a toothpick? A grown-up can help you roll up a toothpick-sized tube of paper and tape it shut.)

1. THE PREPARATION

Place the toothpick along the back of your thumb. Then, tape the toothpick to the back of your thumbnail.

2. THE SETUP

Bend all your fingers in so that it looks like you're holding the toothpick up straight. Make sure your index finger covers the tape.

DEAR GROWN-UP, I quit magic. When I was a kid, I performed a magic show for my classmates. But when a ball I'd made disappear accidentally came back into view, I thought magic wasn't for me! I didn't realize that I just needed practice. If only I was as lucky as Mila and had a mentor like Ms. Greta McGee! My goal with this book is to show kids how much practice and focus it takes to become great at magic, or any interest they'd like to pursue. The book also models the importance of asking for help.

3. THE MOVE

Quickly open both hands to show they are empty! The toothpick will be hidden behind your thumb, and your audience will think it has disappeared! Right before you open your hands, you can say "Hocus Pocus!"

4. THE FINISH

Make the toothpick reappear! Reach your hand up and pretend you are catching the toothpick from the sky. Bend your thumb to make the toothpick reappear. Make sure your index finger covers the tape.

5. THE PRACTICE

Practice a lot in front of the mirror. Make sure that the toothpick and tape aren't seen by mistake. Then, practice your trick for a grown-up you trust. Ask if they have suggestions to improve how you do it, like Ms. McGee helped me!

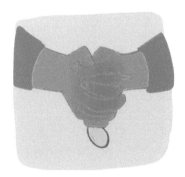

BEND A SPOON!

Grab a spoon at dinner, and bend it in half! Your family will be amazed by how strong you are...especially when you straighten the spoon back out again!

ASK YOUR GROWN-UP TO VISIT WWW.AMYKIMLAT.COM/MAGIC SO YOU CAN LEARN THIS MAGIC TRICK!

So as a first-time author, I'm asking YOU for help. If you and your kid magician love this book, would you consider leaving an honest review on Amazon or with your favorite online retailer? Your review will help this book be discovered, so that you might inspire the next great kid magician!

And what could be more magical than that?

AMY KIMLAT
AUTHOR & FORMER KID MAGICIAN

CPSIA information can be obtained
at www.ICGtesting.com
Printed in the USA
BVHW021522211022
649979BV00009B/656